PEGASUS ENCYCLOPEDIA LIBRARY

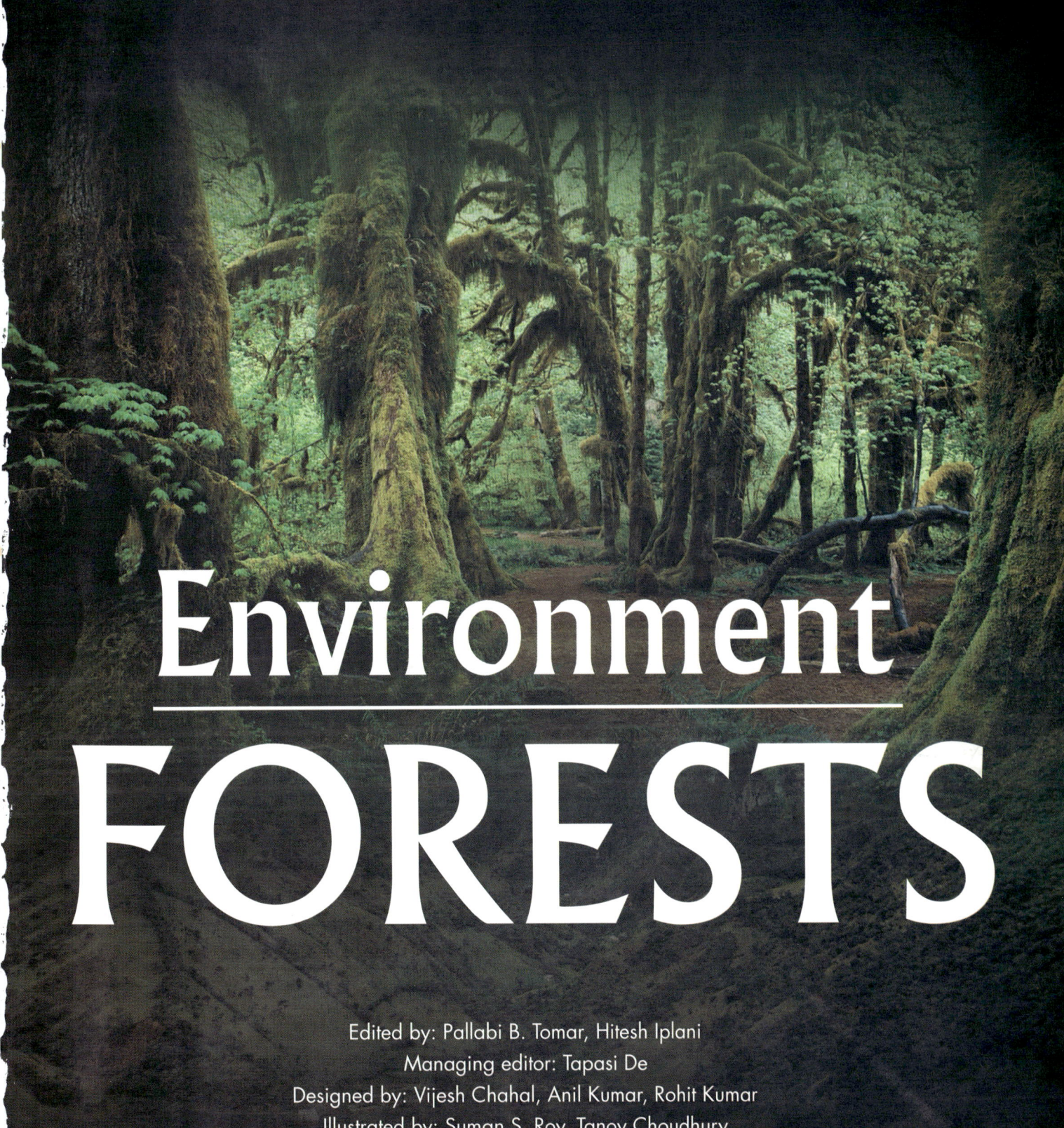

Environment
FORESTS

Edited by: Pallabi B. Tomar, Hitesh Iplani
Managing editor: Tapasi De
Designed by: Vijesh Chahal, Anil Kumar, Rohit Kumar
Illustrated by: Suman S. Roy, Tanoy Choudhury
Colouring done by: Vinay Kumar, Kiran Kumari & Pradeep Kumar

CONTENTS

What are forests? 3

Distribution of forests 5

Types of forests 6

The layers of a forest 11

Forest life 14

Importance of forests 15

Forest products and their uses 17

Threats to forests 20

Conservation of forests 22

Some well-known forests 24

Test Your Memory 31

Index 32

What are forests?

The forest is an area consisting mainly of trees that have formed a safeguard for the Earth to protect life forms. The trees which make up the main area of the forest create a special surrounding which, in turn, affects the kinds of animals and plants that can exist in the forest. Over 30 percent of the Earth's surface is covered with forests.

Of all the ecosystems, forests are the home to the largest number of species on the continent and provide important environmental functions, such as the conservation of biodiversity and the protection of water and soil. The science concerned with the study, preservation, and management of forests is called **forestry**.

Astonishing fact

An area of a rainforest (the size of a football field) is being destroyed each second.

FORESTS

They are also among the most notable storehouses of biological diversity on the land. Forests are the home to around two-thirds of all plant and animal species found on land as well as millions of people who depend on them for their survival. They are vitally important to the health of our planet, especially when it comes to regulating the climate.

Forests have always been important in folklores and worshipped in ancient religions. However, forests are disappearing fast as human populations have increased over the past several thousand years, bringing deforestation, pollution, and industrial usage problems.

Astonishing fact

Trees quite literally form the foundations of many natural systems. They help to conserve soil and water, control avalanches, prevent desertification, protect coastal areas and stabilize sand dunes.

Distribution of forests

Forests cover almost one-third of the world's land area or 3869 million hectares, of which 95 per cent is natural forest and 5 per cent is planted forest. Forests are distributed unevenly across the globe with 17 per cent in Africa, 14 per cent in Asia, 27 per cent in Europe, 14 per cent in North and Central America, 23 per cent in South America and 5 per cent in Oceania.

Two-thirds of the world's forest is currently distributed among 10 countries such as in the Russian Federation, Brazil, Canada, USA, China, Australia, the Democratic Republic of Congo, Indonesia, Angola and Peru.

Astonishing fact

The forests of Central Africa are home to more than 8,000 different species of plants.

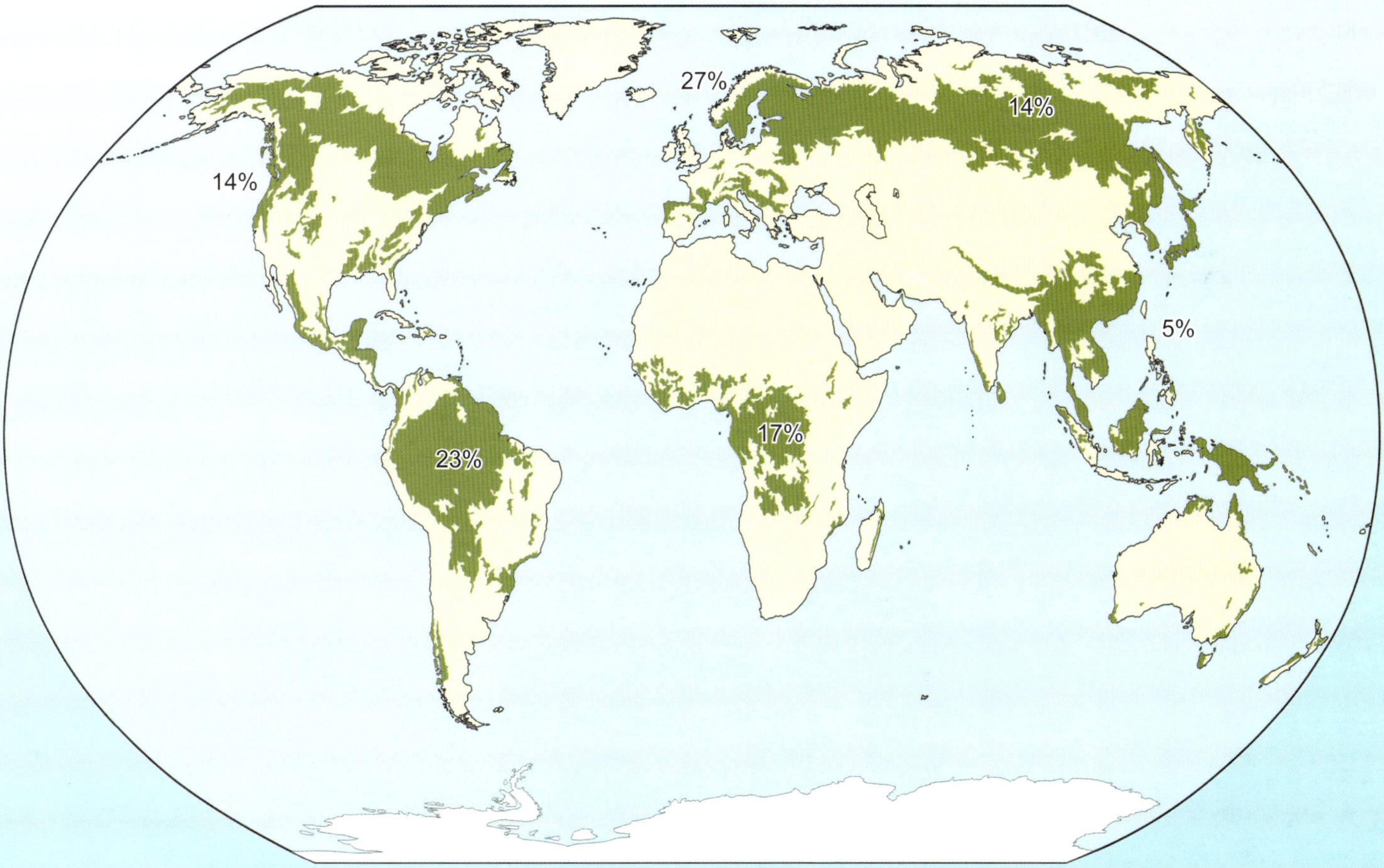

Forests of the World

Types of forests

The type of forest depends mainly on location; that is, distance from equator and altitude and climate. Broadly, forests maybe classified as follows:

Tropical Rainforests

Tropical rainforests are warm, wet forests with many tall trees. In most tropical rainforests, it rains every day. They are found in Africa, Asia, Australia, and South and Central America. Tropical rainforests are home to a huge number of different plants and animals. All tropical rainforests are endangered.

Rainforests need lots of water and most of it comes pouring down as it rains at least 200 cm per year. Some tropical rainforests get more than 3 cm rain per day! When it is not raining, the leaves drip and steam rises. This keeps the whole rainforest constantly wet and steamy.

Rainforests now cover less than 6 per cent of the Earth's land surface. Scientists estimate that more than half of all the world's plant and animal species live in tropical rain forests. Tropical rainforests produce 40 per cent of the Earth's oxygen.

Mangrove Forests

Mangrove forests thrive near the mouths of large rivers where river deltas provide lots of sediment (sand and mud). Mangrove roots collect sediments and slow the water's flow, helping to protect the coastline and preventing erosion. Over time, the roots can collect enough debris and mud to extend the edge of the coastline further out.

Mangrove forests are teeming with life. They are nesting grounds of hundreds of species of birds. They're home to manatees, monkeys, turtles, fish, monitor lizards and in parts of Asia, the fishing cat.

Mangroves exist in more than two-thirds of the saltwater coast areas of tropical and subtropical Africa, Asia, Australia and North and South America. They're found only in a thin fringe right along the coast.

Astonishing fact

The water in a mangrove swamp is so salty it would kill most plants. But the roots of red mangroves contain a waxy substance that helps keep the salt out.

Temperate Forests

Temperate forests are often called **deciduous forests**. One of the most interesting features of the temperate deciduous forest is its changing seasons. The word 'deciduous' means exactly what the leaves on these trees do—change colour in autumn, fall off in the winter, and grow back again in the spring. This adaptation helps trees in the forest survive winter.

Temperate deciduous forests are found in the middle latitudes around the globe and have four distinct seasons—spring, summer, fall and winter. In the northern hemisphere, these forests are found in North America, Europe and Asia. In the southern hemisphere, there are smaller areas of these forests in South America, Africa, and Australia.

Temperate forests are almost always made of two types of trees, deciduous and evergreen. Deciduous trees are trees that lose their leaves in the winter. Evergreens are trees that keep their leaves all year long like the pine trees. Forests can either have deciduous trees, evergreens, or a combination of both.

Astonishing fact

Temperate forests cover about 8.3 million square km of the Earth's surface.

Mangrove Forests

Mangrove forests thrive near the mouths of large rivers where river deltas provide lots of sediment (sand and mud). Mangrove roots collect sediments and slow the water's flow, helping to protect the coastline and preventing erosion. Over time, the roots can collect enough debris and mud to extend the edge of the coastline further out.

Mangrove forests are teeming with life. They are nesting grounds of hundreds of species of birds. They're home to manatees, monkeys, turtles, fish, monitor lizards and in parts of Asia, the fishing cat.

Mangroves exist in more than two-thirds of the saltwater coast areas of tropical and subtropical Africa, Asia, Australia and North and South America. They're found only in a thin fringe right along the coast.

Astonishing fact

The water in a mangrove swamp is so salty it would kill most plants. But the roots of red mangroves contain a waxy substance that helps keep the salt out.

FORESTS

Temperate Forests

Temperate forests are often called **deciduous forests**. One of the most interesting features of the temperate deciduous forest is its changing seasons. The word 'deciduous' means exactly what the leaves on these trees do—change colour in autumn, fall off in the winter, and grow back again in the spring. This adaptation helps trees in the forest survive winter.

Temperate deciduous forests are found in the middle latitudes around the globe and have four distinct seasons—spring, summer, fall and winter. In the northern hemisphere, these forests are found in North America, Europe and Asia. In the southern hemisphere, there are smaller areas of these forests in South America, Africa, and Australia.

Temperate forests are almost always made of two types of trees, deciduous and evergreen. Deciduous trees are trees that lose their leaves in the winter. Evergreens are trees that keep their leaves all year long like the pine trees. Forests can either have deciduous trees, evergreens, or a combination of both.

Astonishing fact

Temperate forests cover about 8.3 million square km of the Earth's surface.

Taiga or Boreal Forest

A taiga is also called a **boreal forest**. The taiga is primarily a coniferous forest (evergreen trees with needles) like the temperate rainforest, but the taiga is located between 50 degrees latitude north and the Arctic Circle. This spans the northern parts of North America, Europe, and Asia. Taiga is a Russian word for marshy pine forest.

The taiga is characterized by a cold, harsh climate, a low rate of precipitation (snow and rain) and short growing season. There are two types of taigas— open woodlands with widely spaced trees and dense forests whose floor is generally in shade.

Many animals make their home in the taiga for at least part of the year. Some stay year-round. In the summer, birds and insects are abundant. Many bird species migrate to the taiga and breed and nest there during summer. Other birds, such as sparrows and crows, stay in the taiga year-round. Mammals include herbivores like rabbits and carnivores such as lynx, wolverines and bobcats.

Lynx

Astonishing fact

The taiga is the largest land biome on Earth. It covers about 28 million square km or 17 per cent of the Earth's land area.

FORESTS

Cloud Forest

A cloud forest is a forest in a region with consistent cloud cover, which actually dip into the forest itself, creating a very moist, misty, dim environment. Some of the most famous cloud forests are in South America, where researchers gather to study the ecology of cloud forests and to promote the preservation of this unique type of forest. South-east Asia and Africa also have large stretches of cloud forest.

Cloud forests often host a great deal of moss and other water-loving plants and epiphytes like orchids. The environment of the cloud forest is definitely unique, hosting a diverse range of plant and animal species, some of which can be found nowhere else in the world. The clouds obscure visibility, especially high up in the forest, and the environment feels very damp. Constant sounds of dripping water can be heard and the forest floor is usually wet in nature. The trees, shrubs and plants grow thick and lush, with an abundance of epiphytic plants growing on every available surface, taking advantage of the huge amounts of moisture in the air to grow and thrive.

Astonishing fact

More than a thousand species of orchids have been found in the cloud forests of Peru alone.

The layers of a forest

Forests often have several distinct layers. They are:

Forest floor

The forest floor is covered with blankets of moss, leaves, twigs, and animal droppings. Some dead animals also end up on the forest floor. The forest floor is where recycling occurs. Fungi, insects, bacteria, and earthworms are among the many organisms that break down waste materials and ready them for reuse and recycling throughout the forest system.

Astonishing fact

More than 2,000 tropical forest plants have been identified by scientists as having anti-cancer properties!

Herb layer

The herb layer is made up of ferns, grasses, wild flowers and other soft-stemmed plants. Like the shrub layer, what is in the herb layer depends on the openness of the canopy and understory. The more open the canopy, the thicker and richer the herb layer. It includes small animals, insects, mice, snakes, turtles and ground nesting birds.

Forest floor

FORESTS

Astonishing fact

The world's boreal forest wraps around the northern hemisphere like a green cloak. This vast ecosystem is easily seen from space and is sometimes referred to as Earth's green halo.

Understory

The understory is made up of shorter trees that are not as tall as the trees in the canopy. It does not provide as many resources as the canopy does, but it does provide shelter and shade for animals. When gaps form in the canopy, often times understory trees take advantage of the opening and grow to fill in the canopy.

Shrub layer

The shrub layer is characterized by woody vegetation that grows relatively close to the ground. Forests that have closed canopies and understory's have less of a shrub layer. Forests with open canopies and understory's have a heavy shrub layer.

Understory

Shrub layer

12

The layers of a forest

Forests often have several distinct layers. They are:

Forest floor

The forest floor is covered with blankets of moss, leaves, twigs, and animal droppings. Some dead animals also end up on the forest floor. The forest floor is where recycling occurs. Fungi, insects, bacteria, and earthworms are among the many organisms that break down waste materials and ready them for reuse and recycling throughout the forest system.

Astonishing fact

More than 2,000 tropical forest plants have been identified by scientists as having anti-cancer properties!

Herb layer

The herb layer is made up of ferns, grasses, wild flowers and other soft-stemmed plants. Like the shrub layer, what is in the herb layer depends on the openness of the canopy and understory. The more open the canopy, the thicker and richer the herb layer. It includes small animals, insects, mice, snakes, turtles and ground nesting birds.

Forest floor

FORESTS

Astonishing fact

The world's boreal forest wraps around the northern hemisphere like a green cloak. This vast ecosystem is easily seen from space and is sometimes referred to as Earth's green halo.

Understory

The understory is made up of shorter trees that are not as tall as the trees in the canopy. It does not provide as many resources as the canopy does, but it does provide shelter and shade for animals. When gaps form in the canopy, often times understory trees take advantage of the opening and grow to fill in the canopy.

Shrub layer

The shrub layer is characterized by woody vegetation that grows relatively close to the ground. Forests that have closed canopies and understory's have less of a shrub layer. Forests with open canopies and understory's have a heavy shrub layer.

Understory

Shrub layer

The layers of a forest

Canopy

Canopy

The canopy is formed by the mass of intertwined branches, twigs, and leaves of the tall, mature trees. The crowns of the dominant trees receive most of the sunlight. This is where most of the tree's food is produced. The canopy forms a shady, protective 'umbrella' over the rest of the forest. Fruit-eating birds, insects and other mammals that eat leaves or fruit live in the canopy.

Emergent layer

The emergent layer exists in the tropical rainforest and is composed of a few scattered trees that tower over the canopy. This layer gets more sun than any other layer in a rainforest.

Astonishing fact

Nearly 90 per cent of the 1.2 billion people living in extreme poverty worldwide depend on forests for their livelihoods.

Emergent layer

FORESTS

Forest life

Forests occupy one third of the Earth's land area and are found on all corners of the globe. The forest is a complex community where trees and other plants and animals live in delicate balance. An enormous variety of creatures inhabit the forest. Some are spectacular, others are hidden somewhere beneath the canopy of countless billions of leaves.

Forest animals vary from area to area. The tropical rainforests contain the greatest diversity of animal species on Earth. Dense growing trees create a thick canopy layer in the tropical rainforests that keep the sun from penetrating the lower layers of the forest. This means that most animals that live here must be adapted to living in the trees. A variety of birds, bats, monkeys, snakes and other animals can be found in tropical rainforests.

Animals living in temperate deciduous forests must be adapted to cold winters. Common species found in temperate deciduous forests include, red fox, hawks, woodpecker and cardinals.

Animals found in boreal forests must be adapted to long, cold winters and usually have thick fur. Deer, moose, elk, caribou, snowshoe hare, wolves, grizzly bears, lynxes and wolverines are some examples.

Importance of forests

People began life on this planet as forest dwellers. They were food gatherers and depended on the forest for all their needs: food, clothing, and shelter. They gradually became food growers, clearing a small patch in the forest to grow food. But they continued to depend on forests to meet a lot of their needs. Even today people depend on the forest for paper, timber, firewood, medicine, and fodder.

Firewood

For the rural population, wood is an important source of energy for cooking and heating. They prefer smaller stems as these are easier to collect and carry. The wood that they select should be easy to split and have low moisture content to dry faster. Some of the wood is converted to charcoal and used for cooking.

Fodder

Fodder from the forest forms an important source for cattle and other grazing animals in the hilly and the arid regions and during a drought. There are many varieties of grasses, trees, and shrubs that are nutritious for the livestock. Care is taken to see that trees poisonous to cattle are not grown. Trees that produce a large crown above the reach of cattle are preferred.

Rainforests are critical in maintaining the Earth's limited supply of drinking and freshwater.

FORESTS

Fencing

Fences created with trees and shrubs are preferred in developing countries as they are cheap to maintain yet give protection. Species that have thorns or are prickly and have stiff branches and leaves that are not edible, are preferred. These species should be fast growing, hardy, and long lived.

Checking soil erosion

Tree roots bind the soil and prevent erosion caused by wind or water. Leaf fall also provides a soil cover that further protects the soil. Casuarina planted along the coastal region has helped in binding the sand and stabilizing the sand dunes in the area.

Soil improvement

Some species of trees have the ability to return nitrogen to the soil through root decomposition or fallen leaves. Such trees are planted to increase the nitrogen content of the soil.

Rainforests act as the world's thermostat by regulating temperatures and weather patterns.

Fencing

The largest temperate rainforests are found on North America's Pacific Coast and stretch from Northern California up into Canada.

Forest products and their uses

Timber

Trees are commercially chopped for timber in different parts of the world. It is used in timber-based industries such as plywood, saw mills, paper and pulp, etc.

Bamboo

Main commercial uses of bamboo are as timber substitutes, fodder and raw material for basket, paper and pulp and other small-scale industries.

Cane

Cane or rattan are the stems of a climber plant and are used for a large number of household items. It is used to make walking sticks, polo sticks, baskets, picture frames, screens, and mats.

Mat

Polo sticks

Fruits

Fruit trees are an important source of income and food for the rural household. In some areas fruit trees are commonly planted along the field borders and around the wells. Mango, coconut, orange, pear, jackfruit and many others grow wild in the forest.

Medicinal use

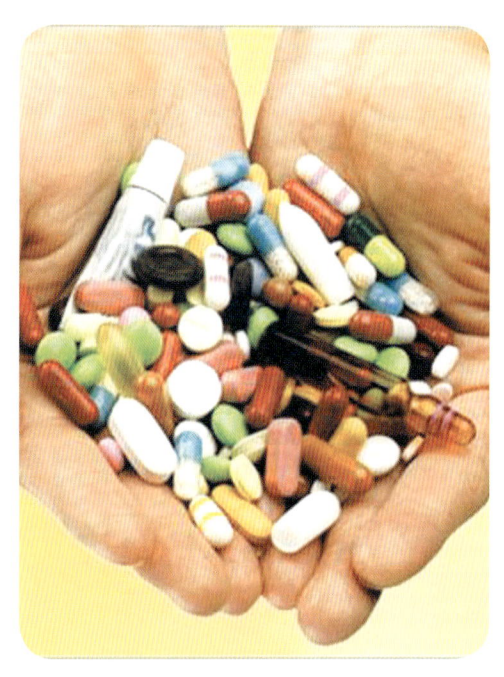

Since time immemorial humans have been depending on the forest to cure them of various ailments. Even today man is dependent on the forest for herbs and plants to fight against disease. Leaves, bark, and other parts of many trees also have medicinal value and are used to make various medicines.

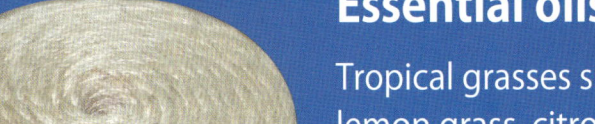

Forest products and their uses

Fibre

Plant fibre has many different uses. Soft fibers such as jute are derived from the stems of the plant. Hard fibre from the leaves of hemp and sisal are used to make fabrics for various applications. Coir, another form of fibre from the fruit of the coconut, is used to make ropes.

Coir

Essential oils

Tropical grasses such as lemon grass, citronella and khus are the source of essential oils. Oil is distilled from the wood of various species such as sandalwood, agar and pine. Oil is also derived from the leaves of certain plants and trees such as eucalyptus, camphor, wintergreen and pine. These oils are used for making soaps, cosmetics, incense, pharmaceuticals and confectionery.

Jute bag

Astonishing fact

The trees of a tropical rainforest are so densely packed that rain falling on the canopy can take as long as 10 minutes to reach the ground.

Eucalyptus tree

Threats to forests

Nearly half of the planet's original forest cover is gone. And much of what remains is in trouble. Diseases and insects are slowly killing the entire species of trees. Illegal logging is impoverishing local people and communities and destroying vital wildlife habitat. Woods have become tinderboxes for destructive fires.

Deforestation and degradation of the world's forests harm communities, economies, plants, animals and the basic ability of forest ecosystems to function and provide services such as fresh water that benefit people everywhere.

Deforestation

Deforestation means the process of removing the trees in forests and woodland and using the land for other purposes. Each year, approximately 32 million acres are lost to deforestation. Illegal logging accounts for much of this loss. Other forests are cut for conversion to agriculture and development.

Many of the forests that remain are severely fragmented, compromised in their ability to shelter wildlife or to supply fresh water to people. Deforestation also contributes 20 to 25 per cent of all carbon pollution causing global climate change and contributes to the impoverishment of forest-dependent communities.

Astonishing fact

80 per cent of the flowers in the Australian rainforests are not found anywhere else in the world.

Threats to forests

Destructive and illegal logging

More and more areas of pristine forest are being cut down to feed timber and paper mills around the world (an area the size of a football pitch disappears every two seconds). Much of this logging is destructive and can also be illegal, particularly in poorer countries where corruption, weak governance and a lack of money make it difficult for the authorities to guard and enforce the law.

Agriculture

Deforestation is also being driven by another human factor— agriculture. Ancient rainforests are being cleared to open up new land for crops such as soya and palm oil, which are grown on an industrial scale to supply the growing demand from food companies across the world.

Climate change

From storing carbon to recycling water into the atmosphere, it's the ancient forests play a critical role in the regulation of the global climate. It is clear that their destruction is a major contributor to the climate change. So protecting our ancient forests from further devastation is absolutely essential if we are serious about tackling climate change.

FORESTS

Astonishing fact

It is noted that every ten years 5-10 per cent of tropical rainforest will be lost!

Conservation of forests

Forests have a vital part to play in boosting the welfare of people and our environment. Conservation of forest includes preserving, protecting the diverse trees, plants, animals and other micro-organisms from turning inactive from the face of the world. Avoiding the wipe-out of the worldwide forests ought to be a major priority to battle global warming.

Forests and plants enable the production of oxygen which we require to live on. They, besides provide home ground for endangered species, clean drinking water and offer economical opportunities.

Methods of conservation of forests

1. Planting of trees or seeds in order to create open land into forest or woodland is termed as **afforestation**. Afforestation prevents the Earth from erosion and helps to maintain water balance. It is a robust generator of wildlife. It helps cool the Earth and rids the air of carbon dioxide, giving out oxygen which is important for life.

Destructive and illegal logging

More and more areas of pristine forest are being cut down to feed timber and paper mills around the world (an area the size of a football pitch disappears every two seconds). Much of this logging is destructive and can also be illegal, particularly in poorer countries where corruption, weak governance and a lack of money make it difficult for the authorities to guard and enforce the law.

Agriculture

Deforestation is also being driven by another human factor— agriculture. Ancient rainforests are being cleared to open up new land for crops such as soya and palm oil, which are grown on an industrial scale to supply the growing demand from food companies across the world.

Climate change

From storing carbon to recycling water into the atmosphere, it's the ancient forests play a critical role in the regulation of the global climate. It is clear that their destruction is a major contributor to the climate change. So protecting our ancient forests from further devastation is absolutely essential if we are serious about tackling climate change.

FORESTS

Conservation of forests

Astonishing fact

It is noted that every ten years 5-10 per cent of tropical rainforest will be lost!

Forests have a vital part to play in boosting the welfare of people and our environment. Conservation of forest includes preserving, protecting the diverse trees, plants, animals and other micro-organisms from turning inactive from the face of the world. Avoiding the wipe-out of the worldwide forests ought to be a major priority to battle global warming.

Forests and plants enable the production of oxygen which we require to live on. They, besides provide home ground for endangered species, clean drinking water and offer economical opportunities.

Methods of conservation of forests

1. Planting of trees or seeds in order to create open land into forest or woodland is termed as **afforestation**. Afforestation prevents the Earth from erosion and helps to maintain water balance. It is a robust generator of wildlife. It helps cool the Earth and rids the air of carbon dioxide, giving out oxygen which is important for life.

Conservation of forests

2. Instruct other people about the importance of the environment and how they can serve in saving forests.
3. Indiscriminate deforestation should be prohibited.
4. Wastage of timber and fuel wood to be avoided.
5. Alternative sources of energy, such as biogas should be used to supplement fuel wood.
6. Forest fires should be prevented.
7. Pests and diseases of the forest trees should be controlled chemically and biologically.
8. Grazing of cattle in forests should be discouraged.
9. Cutting of trees should be prohibited.
10. Reforestation (re-planting) of the deforested areas should be encouraged.

Astonishing fact

Before 1500 A.D., there were approximately 6 million native people living in the Brazilian Amazon. But as the forests disappeared, so did the people. In the early 1900s, there were less than 250,000 native people living in the Amazon.

Some well-known forests

Amazon Rainforest

Few forests are as well-known as the Amazon Rainforest which is also known as Amazonia or the Amazon Jungle. It is one of the world's greatest natural resources. As its vegetation continuously recycles carbon dioxide into oxygen, it is often described as the 'Lungs of our planet'. About 20 percent of Earth's oxygen is produced by the Amazon rainforest! The Amazon Rainforest covers two-fifths of South America, spreading across parts of nine countries such as Brazil, Colombia, Peru, Venezuela, Ecuador, Bolivia, Guyana, Suriname and French Guiana.

The Amazon Rainforest has the greatest collection of plant and animal life. 1 in 10 species from around the world are found in the Amazon. The Amazon Jungle is home to approximately 427 species of mammals, 378 reptiles, 428 amphibians, 1,294 birds, 3,000 fish, 40,000 plants and 2.5 million insect species!

Sherwood Forest

Sherwood Forest is world famous for being the hideaway home of the medieval folk hero, Robin Hood. It is a royal forest in Nottinghamshire, England.

Large sections of the forest were felled in medieval times, but areas of the forest still survive today, including the Major Oak where Robin Hood is reputed to have made his hideout.

Legend tells that Robin and his band of outlaws hunted the royal deer and robbed 'rich' noblemen passing through the forest. They often passed on their booty to the poor residents of the area.

The Major Oak is said to be at least 1000 years and weighs a massive 23 tons. More than 900 of the trees in the park are over 600 years old and the forest is rich in wildlife.

FORESTS

Black Forest

Black Forest is one of the greatest forests in the world. Located in the south-west corner of the state of Baden-Württemberg, Germany, the Black Forest borders France, Switzerland, and the Neckar River.

This forest acquired its name due to a large concentration of pine trees which causes it to look quite dark from a distance. Additionally, the nearby mountains can cast their shadows over the valleys and further serve to darken it.

The Black Forest region is one of Germany's most popular tourist destinations. The Black Forest combines great outdoor scenery with unique local customs and products. It is also the heart of Germany's timber and woodworking industry that generates much of the region's economy beyond tourism.

Astonishing fact

Temperate rainforests used to exist on almost every continent in the world, but today only 50 per cent (75 million acres) of these forests remain worldwide.

Some well-known forests

Bialowieza Forest

Bialowieza Primeval Forest is located in Poland straddling the border between Belarus and Poland. On the Polish side it is partly protected as a National Park and occupies over 100 sq km. The border between the two countries runs through the forest and is closed for large animals and tourists for the time being.

Today Bialowieza Forest is perhaps best known as forming an enclave for the European bison. The attempts to rescue this huge mammal, once a common sight there was considered a success in 1952 when the first specimens were released back into the wild.

FORESTS

Virgin Komi Forests

The Virgin Komi Forests form the first UNESCO World Heritage Site declared in Russia in 1995. It is one of the largest virgin boreal forests still surviving in Europe. For more than 50 years the plant-life, rivers, lakes of the area have been carefully studied and they provide insight into the natural process which affect the taiga biodiversity (types of life forms in a particular area).

Astonishing fact

More than 145,039 square km of natural forest are lost each year.

Russia's Virgin Komi Forests have the status of a National Park. Located in the Northern Ural Mountains, the heritage site includes some 32, 800 sq km of virgin boreal forest. The Komi Forest is a real treasury of taiga. This area is the home of more than 40 mammal species, 204 bird species and 16 fish species.

Astonishing fact

Less than 1 per cent of the tropical rainforest have been studied for their medicinal uses. The rest of it still remains untouched.

Some well-known forests

Hoh Rainforest

The Hoh Rainforest is a part of the Olympic National Park, which is in turn located in Washington State's Olympic Peninsula. As one of the few temperate rainforests in the United States, and one of the largest, the forest is unique in U.S. Sitka Spruce and Western Hemlock are the dominant species of the area.

Throughout the winter season, rain falls frequently in the Hoh Rainforest, contributing to the yearly total of 140 to 170 inches of rainfall each year. The result is a lush, green canopy of both coniferous and deciduous species. Mosses and ferns that blanket the surfaces add another dimension to the enchantment of the rainforest.

FORESTS

Laurisilva of Madeira

The Laurisilva lies between 300 and 1300 m altitude on the island of Madeira. The forest extends across 22,100 hectares of land. It covers roughly 16 per cent of the island's surface, making the Madeira Laurisilva one of the largest forests of its kind in the world.

The most important feature of the Madeira Laurisilva is not only the extensive wealth of biodiversity of the forest, but also its exceptionally high level of endemic (typical to a place) species. For example, the remarkable and high quality hard wood trees available, including the valuable Til, Vinhático, Barbosano, Aderno, Pau Branco and Folhado trees. Another 66 known species of plants are entirely endemic to Madeira, including the Uveira da Serra and Urze species (brush plants).

The 'Godiera da Madeira' or 'Goodyera Macrophylla'—an orchid, is an example of one of the rare and endemic flowers species found almost exclusively in the Laurisilva.

More than 500 endemic species of invertebrate also form a part of the Laurisilva, including many molluscs, insects and spiders. Some of the well-known endemic vertebrates include the Long Toed Wood Pigeon and two rare species of bats.

Long toed wood pigeon

Test Your MEMORY

1. What are forests?

2. How are forests distributed?

3. Name the types of forests.

4. Write two sentences about Cloud Forests.

5. Name the different layers of a forest.

6. Write two sentences about the canopy of a forest.

7. Write about the animals living in a forest.

8. Write two uses of forests.

9. How are forests threatened?

10. Write two forest conservation methods.

11. Why the Amazon Rainforest is called the 'Lungs of our Planet'?

12. Write the names of two well-known forests.

FORESTS

Index

A
adaptation 8
afforestation 22
altitude 6, 30

B
Boreal forest 9, 12, 14, 28, 29

C
canopy 11, 12, 13, 14, 19, 29
climate 4, 5, 6, 7, 9, 20, 21
Cloud forest 10
Coniferous forest 9

D
Deciduous forests 8, 14
deforestation 4, 20, 21, 23

E
ecology 10
ecosystems 3, 12, 20
emergent layer 13
epiphytes 10
equator 6
erosion 7, 16, 22

F
forest floor 10, 11
forestry 3

H
herb layer 11

L
latitudes 8

M
Mangrove forests 7

N
northern hemisphere 8, 12

O
oxygen 6, 22, 24

P
pollution 4, 20
precipitation 9

S
sediments 7
shrub layer 11, 12
southern hemisphere 8

T
Taiga 9, 28
Temperate forests 8
Tropical rainforests 6

U
understory 11, 12

---

* Maps not to scale; for illustration purpose only.